ROCKY FOR GOD

ROCKY FOR GOD

Joseph Marcoguiseppe

Library of Congress Control Number: 2002094196
ISBN :   Hardcover   978-1-4010-7284-1
                 Softcover   978-1-4010-7283-4

To order additional copies of this book, contact:
Xlibris Corporation
1-888-795-4274
www.Xlibris.com
Orders@Xlibris.com
16328

TO JOSEPH

THE ULTIMATE PRIZE FIGHT

A FIGHT FOR MIND, BODY, AND
SOUL

FOR STAGE PLAYS

DOWNSTAGE   STAGE AREA CLOSEST TO AUDIENCE

UPSTAGE   STAGE AREA FURTHEST AWAY FROM AUDIENCE

CENTER STAGE   MIDDLE AREA OF STAGE

STAGE LEFT   TO THE ACTOR'S LEFT WHEN FACING AUDIENCE

STAGE RIGHT   TO THE ACTOR'S RIGHT WHEN FACING AUDIENCE

CHARACTERS

FIGHTER
MAN
RING ANNOUNCER
FIGHT ANNOUNCER

ACT I

Scene I

TIME: The Present

SETTING: Old, weathered looking boxing gym. Center stage . . . the Ring. Beat up lockers, punching bag, exercise floor and wall mats, wall pulleys, garbage cans, fight posters, etc. Heavy bag at upstage right on a raised platform. Stage right, viewer seating area . . . aged, dark wooden connecting seats 5 rows high (quite vertical), 5 to 6 seats per row. Fairly high above the ring are three flat gray light fixtures, each containing a single light bulb (ring lights off at this time). The FIGHTER, with robe draped around his shoulders and towel over his head, is sitting on his stool in the upstage left corner of the ring. He is wearing solid black boxing trunks. The stage is dimly lit as audience enters the theater.

AT RISE: Stage lights go off as ring lights go up illuminating the ring, although still gloomy. After a few moments, FIGHTER stands and begins to shadow box around the ring (no boxing gloves, hands taped). He sheds his robe and towel and continues . . .

FIGHTER
Dig . . . Dig . . . Bang hard. Left . . . Left . . .
Come on, left. Bang with the left. Both hands . . .

(bends and moves throwing body punches)

Beat the body, the head will fall . . . Beat the body.
Beat the body. Beat the body . . .

(Progressively louder with more movement,
FIGHTER has moved across the ring to the
opposite corner and is working hard against a
fictitious opponent. The FIGHTER grabs the top
rope and knees the fictitious opponent in the mid-
section several times.)

How's that! . . . Spit your blood . . . Spit it . . . Spit
it, man.

(MAN enters upstage left pushing broom, pauses
to watch.)

MAN
You'z sure some dirty fighter.

FIGHTER
(startled)
Huh? . . . Huh? . . . Who's there? (stage lights go
up full) . . . Who the hell are you?

MAN
I'z nobody, man . . . I'z just cleans up dis place.

FIGHTER

You're not supposed to be here. No one is. I bought this hole out for the day. Now go on and get the hell outta here.

MAN

I'z gots to do my job.

FIGHTER
(angered)
You ain't gotta do nothin . . . Get outta here.

MAN

Ought not to talk to me like dat. I ain't doin you no harm.

(talks to himself as he continues to sweep)

No right to talk to me like dat . . . no right. I'z just doin whats I gots to do.

FIGHTER

How'd you get in here?

MAN

I tolls you . . . I'z the clean up man.

FIGHTER

Look . . . no one can get in here. No one! I changed the locks and locked every way.

(moves to water bucket by stool, takes keys out of bucket)

I got the only set of keys.

(slams keys down into water bucket)

MAN

I tolls you . . .

FIGHTER
(interrupting)

Who sent you?

(climbs through the ropes and descends from ring)

MAN

Boss Man sent me.

FIGHTER

Who's your Boss Man?

MAN

Boss Man runs the place . . . Runs a whole lot of things.

(FIGHTER moves toward MAN, now down-stage.)

FIGHTER

He does, huh . . . (slowly) . . . Your Boss Man got a name?

MAN
(smiles)

Boss Man got a whole bunch of names.

FIGHTER
(infuriated)
I'll bust your face, Jack . . . right here . . . right now!

(MAN puts his head down and shakes it as if to say, "No" . . . resumes sweeping in a small area where he stands.)

(FIGHTER backs off slowly and moves upstage right to the heavy bag and begins to bang it. After a few moments, he asks . . .)

What's your name?

MAN
(softly)
Rocky.

FIGHTER
(demanding)
I can't hear you!

MAN
(stands erect)
Rocky!

FIGHTER
(laughs)
Rocky? Who . . . ah . . . what . . . Marciano? (no response) . . . Graziano? Or maybe it's Balboa!

(grunts a few bars from Rocky movie theme song)

MAN
(angered)
Rocky! That's it!

(FIGHTER climbs back into ring; begins to
shadow box.)

FIGHTER
You've got a last name . . . right? Everybody's got
a last name.

MAN
Never got one.

FIGHTER
Never got one?

(MAN resumes sweeping and shakes his head as if
to say, "No.")

You a fighter?

MAN
Never fought 'round here.

FIGHTER
I don't mean here . . . in this dump. I mean you
ever fight before . . . prize fight . . . profession-
ally, anywhere . . . you know . . . in the world?

MAN
I fought the best all over the world.

FIGHTER
You did . . . huh. Ever fought in the Garden?

MAN
What garden?

FIGHTER
(stops)
What Garden! You from Mars, man. The Garden . . . Madison Square Garden . . . New York City.

MAN
Not dat garden. (pauses, smiles) . . . That first garden . . . long, long dime age. That (slowly) . . . that p l e a s a n t garden. (pauses, more serious now) . . . But, only nears the end. Lost dat one.

FIGHTER
What happened?

MAN
Oh . . . I guess I juss didn't have whad it took. I thought I was ready. My first Main Event.

(moves center stage, leans broom against the ring)

I trained hard, real hard. I was groomed, ya know . . . hand picked. (begins to spar) . . . I had the bess trainer . . . brought me 'round real slow . . . carefully, not too fast. But . . . but . . . but then . . . in DAT FITE, I was counter punchin . . . waiting for my opponent to lead me . . . so I could counter punch. But, I kept gettin hit (MAN starts taking punches) and . . . and . . . I . . . I move and kep gettin hit. So I jab and move . . . jab, jab . . . jab and move . . . getting hit again and again. (pause) . . . I went after him . . . moved in widh hooks and combinations (MAN fighting feverishly now) gettin my shots, but most were glazin . . . and glancin. I . . . I . . . couldn't hit him square. Then he backs me up against the ropes (MAN now against outer ring ropes) and the punches were comin from all directions. I tried turnin 'im. I juss culdn't do it. I'z gettin hit solid punches. Left . . . right . . . left, left . . . right. I started bangen, bangen . . . dats all I'z culd do. Didn't matter. I got hit . . . got hit . . . you know, gots hit . . . hit . . . hit . . . hits again . . .

(MAN reels off ropes falling to floor, semi-conscious.)

(FIGHTER laughs, climbs out of ring and moves to MAN.)

FIGHTER
You sure are one punch drunk ol' fool.

(picks MAN up)

Let's get yo ass up.

(MAN staggers up and is led over to seating section, stage right, where he sits. FIGHTER

towels MAN's face, then walks to downstage left
outer ring area.)

Hey, Ol' Man . . . that sure was some fight you
had there.

MAN
You think you so bad. You ain't nothin.

FIGHTER
(laughs)
I ain't, huh.

MAN
Nothin.

(FIGHTER goes back in ring and shadow boxes.)

FIGHTER
Let me tell you something 'bout me. I'm a con-
tender . . . fought many Main Events, and in the
Garden, too . . . Madison Square Garden.

MAN
You'z washed up. Way pass yo prime.

FIGHTER
(stops boxing, reacts angrily)
You don't know Jack crap about me!

MAN
I knows everythin 'bout you. You'z retired, man.
Said so lass month.

FIGHTER
Where'd you get that!

MAN
You knows I'z talkin right.

FIGHTER
Where'd you hear I retired . . . I didn't tell no-body!

MAN
Tolls yoself.

FIGHTER
(shows off foot speed, Ali shuffle)
Do I look retired?

MAN
(angrily)
YOU TOLLS YOSELF!

FIGHTER
You can't know that!

(moves to MAN, grabs top rope closest to MAN)

No one knows that. NO ONE!

MAN
Hmm . . . (as MAN looks away)

FIGHTER
Look at me. What do you know about me?

MAN

I know you're die'n.

(Petrified, FIGHTER turns away and walks to
opposite side of ring and grabs the top rope with
his back to the MAN. FIGHTER slumps a bit.
His head is down.)

FIGHTER

Ol' Man . . . Ol' Man . . .

MAN
(proudly)

Call me, Rocky!

FIGHTER

Rocky . . . (turns and faces MAN) . . . Who are
you?

MAN
(stands)

I'm ROCKY . . . (pauses) . . . ROCKY FOR
GOD!

(FIGHTER slowly walks across ring toward the
MAN.)

FIGHTER

You lost your mind, Jack . . . too many blows to
the head. You ain't no Rocky for God 'cause there
is no God.

MAN

Now who's the fool?

FIGHTER
(quickly)

There ain't no Go . . .

MAN
(interrupting)

No! . . . There is a God! He dhe Boss Man. My Boss Man . . . Yo Boss Man. And I'm his Fighter. His Champion.

(MAN slowly moves upstage, clockwise around the outside of the ring, as he talks to the FIGHTER, almost turning him around in a circle.)

An he sent me here for another fight. (pause) . . . You see I did lose dat first fight. But I won a whole lot of fights after dat. I'm a True Champion. I fought thousands of fights . . . tens of thousands of fights through the years. An I win most of 'em . . . maybe 90% . . .

FIGHTER
(interrupting)

Ninety percent?

MAN
(ignores, continues)

But, dose 10% I lose . . . they make noise . . . they pain . . . they mess widh things. They hurts people . . . Boss Man's people. But Boss Man don't gets down on me when I lose. Unh uh . . . He stays in my corner . . . brings me back to camp to re-train (begins light shadow boxing as he walks) . . . get myself in shape for dhe nex fite. And I win . . . and I win again . . . an I win until I lose. (angered) . . . An I ain't gonna lose here. (stops and points at FIGHTER) You hear what I'm sayin fool. I ain't gonna lose to no bum . . . and you'z a bum!

FIGHTER
(angered)
Get your ass in here.

MAN
Oh, I'm comin.

FIGHTER
Get in here crazy man.

MAN
You'll knows when I'm comin.

(MAN downstage facing audience, back to FIGHTER)

FIGHTER
What you tryin to tell me, Ol' Man . . . that you came here to fight me?

MAN
I came here to kick yo a . . . (stops) . . . to whoop your bu . . . (stops) . . . to beat the livin sh . . . (stops) . . . Teach you a lesson.

FIGHTER

You got nothin to teach me . . . Nothin! Your brains are scrambled . . . fried.

MAN

I don't, huh . . . (turns to FIGHTER) . . . Well, how come you come here to die?

FIGHTER

Hey . . . man, you don't know what the hell you're talkin about.

MAN

You'z a suicide freak.

FIGHTER

(angered)

Don't talk to me.

(FIGHTER turns from MAN and walks across the ring.)

MAN

You hears what I said.

FIGHTER

Shut your mouth.

MAN

A S U I C I D E freak . . . Jack. (walks toward ring)

(FIGHTER moves to ring corner upstage left, leans on ropes with back to MAN.)

FIGHTER

Stay away from me.

MAN

Now, I'z comin in. (MAN climbs into ring.) You think he'll let you be Champion. He lies! He's the King of lies . . . The Heavyweight Champion of lies. He's gonna take your best shots . . . gonna take all you got . . . and pile you up in the middle of this here ring . . . And you gonna DIE.

FIGHTER
(confused)

Look . . . Look . . . So maybe you do know somethin about me . . . maybe you followed my career . . . investigated my life . . . some kind of fight groupie. But, you don't know nothin about why I'm here.

MAN

I knows everythin about why you'z here. See, I knows you . . . knows everythin about you . . . National Golden Gloves Runner-Up . . . (FIGHTER acting proudly, looking at audience) . . . Silver Medallist in the Olympics . . . Then, you tun Pro . . . became dhe 8th ranked Light Heavyweight in the world. Fought for the title once . . . and got yourself knocked out in the second round. (FIGHTER is deflated.) Never was a Champion. Now, yo too ol' . . . Can't get a title fight . . . and don't want one . . . 'cause you knows you gets whooped again. So you'z come here to die.

FIGHTER

That's where you're wrong. I came here to live . . .
To be Champion. I'm gonna show the whole
world who I am!

MAN
(shaking his head in disgust)
And you givs up yowl soul fo it.

FIGHTER

I'll give up nothin.

MAN

Youz throws aways everything . . .

FIGHTER
(interrupting)
That's what I . . . noth . . .

MAN
(interrupting)
Everythin . . . gone . . . wast . . . ed . . .

FIGHTER
(grabs MAN center ring)
Nothin . . . You hear me . . . Nothin.

MAN
(struggling)
You still won'ts be Champ.

FIGHTER
(crazed, jostling MAN about)
I will be . . . I will be . . . (stops) . . . I WILL BE!

MAN
(shaken, insists)
YOU WON'TS BE! He won't let you! HE
HATES YOU, SON! (FIGHTER releases
MAN, moves away.) HATES YOU . . . Despises
you. Yeah, that's right. He gonna promise you
the belt. Promise you all kinds of things . . . A
PLACE IN FIGHT GAME HISTORY. But, you
be no Champ . . . 'cause he hates you . . . Hates
everybody. You be jumpin up an down, going
all kins of ways . . . jammin junk up your nose . . .
all wide eyed and crazy. Then . . . then . . . he
gonna kill you, and you dies forever. Like I says
befo . . . you'z a suicide freak!

FIGHTER
(angered)
That's enough of that bullshit talk from you. I
make my deal TODAY. I get my edge TO-
DAY . . . the edge I never had. It's my turn now.
(MAN gestures disapproval) . . . No more second
place finishes. No more tank joints like this dump.
No more jive trainers . . . dive motels . . . penny
ass fights. No! . . . DAMN NO! I'm gonna play
the game . . . gonna roll the dice (gestures) and
play the game with the Man . . . (laughs cra-
zily) . . . the BOSS MAN . . . (continues to
laugh) . . .

(MAN lunges at FIGHTER and spins him
around.)

MAN
Don't you calls him the Boss Man . . . 'cause he

ain't no Boss Man. HE'S A PUNK! You call him by his real name . . . SATAN . . . that's right . . . get used to it. Satan, the Evil One. He's comin here to tear up yo soul . . . split you wide open. An you ain't gots no defense.

FIGHTER
(still laughing)
Don't want one.

MAN
You'z gonna needs one . . . A Master Defense . . . juss like . . .

FIGHTER
(interrupting)
And who's gonna give me one . . . you? (ridicules) . . . You gonna save me, Ol' Man. (serious) . . . Even if I wanted a defense from him . . . which I don't . . . you'd be the last fool I'd look to. Some sorry, broken down . . . fortune tellin freak. Yeah, you're the freak. Talkin all that high and mighty, holly roller crystal ball bullshit. Huh . . . Rocky For God. Your Boss Man don't exist . . . You don't exist. You the lie! (pause) . . . L I A R!!!

MAN
(demanding)
You believes in the Evil One . . . But not GOD!

FIGHTER
There ain't no God, fool. And there ain't no you . . . not who you think you are.

(MAN changes demeanor/speech pattern, now
preacher-like.)

MAN

And, Oh . . . what a glorious God He is . . . Such
a praise-worthy, God. This great Father of
ours . . . who gives us our gifts and our good-
ness . . . our treasures and our joys. And per-
mits . . . through His all-merciful, redemptive
love (now points to FIGHTER) such lower forms
of intelligence to exist. My . . . My . . . can there
be any question of the magnificence of His
Thrown . . . The beauty of His Being. Praise the
Lord . . . Praise God, The Almighty . . .

FIGHTER
(interrupting)

Hold it . . .

MAN
(continuing)

For in His Wisdom . . . His D I V I N E . . . Wisdom . . . He sent His only begotten Son . . . Jesus
Christ . . .

FIGHTER
(interjecting)

Oh . . . Jesus . . .

MAN
(continues)

To show us the way . . . The only way . . . Help-
ing us through this darkness . . .

FIGHTER
(interrupting)
Hold it . . . Hold it . . .

MAN
(ignores, never stops)
When we are disbelievers (ad libs) . . .

FIGHTER
(insistently)
Hold it! Enough!

(grabs MAN and pushes him into the ropes stage
right, shaking him as MAN continues to ad lib) . . .

MAN
Saving wretches all the time (ad libs) . . .

FIGHTER
(yelling now, almost choking MAN)
Hold it! . . . Hold it! . . . Hold it! . . .

MAN
(yelling simultaneously)
Our good Lord, Jesus Christ! (ad libs) . . .

FIGHTER
(screaming now)
HOLD IT! . . . HOLD IT! . . . HOLD IT! . . .

MAN
(screaming simultaneously)
God graces us with Angels from Heaven above!
(ad libs) . . .

(FIGHTER SCREAMING . . . feverishly shaking
MAN. MAN SCREAMING . . . looking to
heavens, continues to ad lib. After a time . . .)

BELL RINGS

(FIGHTER and MAN stop. Long pause. Both
visibly shaken. FIGHTER staggers to his corner
and sits on his stool, upstage left ring area. He
places robe over his shoulders. MAN stumbles/
exits through the ropes stage right, locates broom
and sweeps [staggering] to downstage left area.
Stage lights go off as ring lights go to dim. MAN
remains in dark, downstage left.)

END SCENE I

SCENE II

SETTING: Same as ending to Scene I with FIGHTER sitting on stool in ring corner upstage left with robe draped over his shoulders. Ring lights overhead are dim. No other lights. MAN is downstage left in the dark standing/leaning on his broom facing the audience. After a long pause . . .

FIGHTER
(looking straight ahead, says in a whisper . . .)
Ol' Man . . . (no response, pause) Ol' Man . . .
(no response)

MAN
(slyly)
You knows my name.

FIGHTER
(reluctantly)
Rocky.

MAN
(gleefully)
Whats you want?

FIGHTER
You some kind of an Angel or somethin?

(overhead spotlight now goes up on MAN)

MAN
Now, you'z beginnin to see dhe light.

FIGHTER
You my Guardian Angel?

MAN
Don't let dhe light blind you, son. It doesn't work dhat way.

(FIGHTER turns his face toward MAN.)

FIGHTER
Tell me how it works.

MAN
Metaphysically speaking . . . protracted problems such as those H I T H E R . . . (points to FIGHTER without turning) . . . require punctilious meditation followed by an unequivocal operative.

FIGHTER
(confused)
What the hell you sayin to me, Ol' Man?

MAN

Sorry, son. I almost forgot the cover I was takin for this here Bout.

(MAN slouches over, exaggerates demeanor/speech pattern.)

Whats I'z sayin ils . . . if we'z gonna whoops the Devil . . . we'z gottsda Think and Act!

(lights go up full)

FIGHTER
(suspiciously)

We do, huh . . .

(FIGHTER stands, throws off robe and moves around the ring . . . pondering.)

Whoop the Devil? Cover for this Bout?

(FIGHTER moves downstage ring, leans on ropes near MAN and asks . . .)

How come you talk differently at times?

(MAN caught off guard, keeps back to FIGHTER.)

MAN

Oh . . . ah . . . disregard that, son. Ah . . . I mean . . . ah . . . I means . . . forgets dat diffren talkin stuff.

FIGHTER

No way, Jack. I know who you are . . . I figured
you out. Talkin in strange tongues . . . why you
know so much about me. (smiling/confident) . . .
You're the Devil, or his agent . . .

MAN

(interrupting, still with back to FIGHTER)
Wrong . . .

FIGHTER

(continuing)
Trying to test me . . . see if I'd back off my deal.
(assuredly) . . . Well, you don't have to worry. I'm
solid on it.

MAN

Wrong! Wrong!

FIGHTER

Yes . . . Right! That's who you are. How else could
you know why I'm here . . . who I came to meet.
No one else knows that but the Devil himself
(points to MAN) . . . And me.

(MAN turns/moves to ring's edge, looks up at
FIGHTER.)

MAN

You refuse to hear the Truth, looking right
straight at the window of God . . . and you refuse.

FIGHTER

You're damn right . . . I refuse. If you ain't from

the Devil, I got no time for you. I got no time for
no God. That world stinks out there . . . It's rot-
ten! Full of beatings! But, no more for me. I'm
gonna give the beatings now . . . all of them. I
make my deal with Mr. Beater . . . and soon now.

MAN
(grabs outside of ring ropes)
You need me, son.

FIGHTER
(shuns)
If you ain't from Mr. BEATER . . . get out! Go
back to your own Boss Man . . . and leave me
alone.

MAN
(angered)
You need me!

FIGHTER
(shouts)
I don't need you! You're a loser . . . been losin for
years . . . losin every day. I caught your drift when
you said you fought in the garden . . . the other
garden, long time ago . . . The Garden of Eden
right? Your first Main Event. Got your ass kicked
then and been getting it kicked ever since.

(MAN climbs ropes and stands on outside ring
apron, downstage.)

MAN
That's not true.

FIGHTER

It is true! You ain't stopped no killin . . . no starvation . . . no rich mothas beatin up on the poor . . . No nothing!

(MAN slowly circles ring apron, moving upstage right to left.)

MAN

What you know about God! . . . all the miracles He works; all the people He works through. I'm tellin you if it weren't for God pushen all of us, your Main Man (sarcastically) Mr. Beee Terr . . . would have got his way long time ago and blew up this planet.

FIGHTER

Yeah, well . . . I don't know about any of that. All I know is that for me . . . this is my last shot at the Title, and I'm gonna take it.

MAN

Don't you see, son . . . the whole world is full of mees . . . Everybody always talkin . . . me . . . me . . . me first. See that's what he relies on . . . looks for in settin up his next victim. Now, don't take offense, but Satan knows you're not very bright . . . knows you're real weak in Godly thoughts and deeds . . . that your selfishness and pride keeps you from seein all the good and beauty in this here world. But, you're important. There's a lot of folks like you, and they're all important. We can't afford to lose you . . . lose no one. You can't go down for the count. Son, you matter. You and everyone else fit into this whole puzzle of life . . . and how you fit in . . . what you do with your life . . . affects how that whole picture puzzle looks . . .

FIGHTER
(interrupting)
Look . . . Look . . . I've got to get ready.

(MAN climbs into ring by FIGHTER, upstage left ring area, and picks up boxing gloves, black, and mouthpiece from bucket under stool. As he laces up the gloves on the FIGHTER, he continues . . .)

MAN
I'm tellin you there's a future to behold . . . a picture of God's glory on earth that will knock your block off. Yes, we have a glimmer of that portrait every day . . . yes, we do. It shines in a smile, in a prayer . . . in every child . . .

FIGHTER
(interrupting)
Hurry up, will you . . . It's almost time . . .

MAN
(continuing)
In the mountains and the streams . . . on the hillsides . . . yes (smiles) . . . and it's in your heart, son.

(MAN sticks mouthpiece in FIGHTER's mouth.)

Especially in your heart.

(MAN exits ring, stays by FIGHTER's corner.
FIGHTER sits on stool.)

Remember, I'm in your corner.

BELL *R I N G S*

(After bell rings, stage lights go off and ring lights
go up full. FIGHTER stands and slowly moves to
center ring ducking/stalking his opponent, whom
he doesn't see at first. Suddenly, FIGHTER
screams . . .)

FIGHTER
Aaaaaaaaahhhhh . . . .

(backs off center ring to corner)

Damn, are you ugly!

MAN
Who you talkin to?

FIGHTER
Him . . .

MAN
Him . . . who?

FIGHTER
(excitedly)
Him! Don't you see 'im?

MAN

No, I don't. I only sees you in dat ring.

FIGHTER

He's right there . . . (pointing across ring) . . . He's so big . . . so damn ugly.

MAN
(calmly)

What's he look like?

FIGHTER
(exasperated)

How come you can't see him? I thought you were an Angel.

MAN
(indignant)

I never said I had X-Ray vision; now, whats he look like?

FIGHTER

He's got . . . how many? . . . he's got seven heads . . .

MAN
(repeats)

Seven heads . . .

FIGHTER

Ten horns . . . aaaaahhhhh . . . and bear's feet . . .

                    MAN
                   (repeats)
Bear's feet . . .

                  FIGHTER
He's got a body like a lizard or dragon or
somethin . . .

                    MAN
How many arms does he have?

                  FIGHTER
Two arms . . . with lion claws.

                    MAN
Two . . . hmm . . . that's good.

                  FIGHTER
               (looks to MAN)
Good!

               (looks back across ring)

And . . . and he's got a lion's mouth.

                    MAN
                   (repeats)
Lion's mouth.

                  FIGHTER
Who is he?

MAN
(ignores, begins to file his nails)
What's he doin?

FIGHTER
Just standin there . . . starin at me . . . (urgently asks . . .) Is he Satan?

MAN
(calmly)
No . . . It's the Beast.

FIGHTER
(frantically)
What . . . who . . . what's the Beast?

MAN
He's Satan's Fighter . . . you might say his own Heavyweight Champ.

FIGHTER
(scared/confused)
Huh . . . wait . . . Unh uh . . . I . . . I come here to make a deal with the Devil . . . not mess with any Beast. Screw this stuff. (backs off) . . .

MAN
It's your party, brother.

(FIGHTER hears a voice coming from the Beast.)

FIGHTER
Huh? . . . What? . . . What? . . . Are you crazy?

MAN

Whats he want?

FIGHTER
(still looking at the Beast)
He says I've got to fight him to be worthy of a deal with Satan.

MAN

Tough luck, Jack.

FIGHTER
(to MAN)
Wait a minute, Ol' Man . . . Ol' Man . . . (MAN ignores) . . . Rocky . . . Rocky . . . I've changed my mind. I don't want no part of this.

MAN

Too late.

FIGHTER

What do you mean too late?

MAN

Can't get out of it, son.

FIGHTER

Bull . . . I gettin the hell out of this ring!

(FIGHTER tries to step through ring ropes several times and each time he is mystically thrown back into the ring crashing to the ring floor. He pleads . . .)

Rocky . . . Rocky . . .

(MAN ignores FIGHTER on ring floor.)

Rocky, for God's sake . . . Help me!

MAN
So . . . You do needs me.

FIGHTER
(still on ring floor)
Yes . . . Yes, help me.

MAN
He hasn't even laid a glove on you.

FIGHTER
(aroused)
That's right . . .

(FIGHTER slowly gets up and bends/stalks the Beast center ring. Suddenly . . . POW! He goes crashing to ring floor from a right to the jaw.)

MAN
(gleefully)
Now he has.

FIGHTER
(angered)
(to MAN) . . . Damn you! (to Beast) . . . Damn you!

(FIGHTER gets up and quickly . . . POW! He

goes crashing to ring floor from a left to the jaw.
Blood is gushing from FIGHTER's mouth as he
crawls to downstage center ropes and kneeling/
hanging on ropes begs MAN, who has moved
downstage left . . .)

Please . . . Please . . . help me . . . HELP ME . . .
Rocky . . . Help me!

MAN
According to my rules?

FIGHTER
Yes, yes . . . anything.

MAN
(firmly)
In the name of GOD!

FIGHTER
(last gasp)
Yes . . .

MAN
(pauses, then orders . . .)
Be gone . . . Beast!

BELL RINGS

Now . . . it's time to train.

(Ring lights fade to dim. MAN exits stage left.)

END SCENE II

SCENE III

SETTING: FIGHTER is sitting on the ring floor, center ring facing the audience, knees somewhat up as he wipes the blood off his face clumsily with his gloved hands. After a long pause . . .

FIGHTER
(mumbling)
What the hell did I get myself into . . . I ain't never gonna survive this (pause) . . . Ah geez . . .

(Offstage, MAN is humming/whistling a happy tune. FIGHTER turns his head about trying to locate area of sound as he continues to wipe blood. Stage lights gradually go up. MAN enters down-stage left. Still humming, he is carrying in his left hand a gray water bucket and across the length of his body a projection screen. A white towel is draped over the MAN's left shoulder. Difficult to handle, the projection screen and the bucket make contact and clang as he walks. FIGHTER, after watching MAN walk across the stage, asks . . .)

Where you been?

(MAN now at downstage right area)

MAN
Huh . . . Oh, just getting some things together.

FIGHTER
(impatiently)
Well . . . what about me?

MAN
(throws towel into ring)
Wipe your face, son.

(FIGHTER retrieves towel and wipes face as MAN starts to set up projection screen, downstage right.)

Do some push-ups.

(FIGHTER finishes toweling off and reluctantly goes to his knees for push-ups; then, realizing the futility of this exercise because he is wearing boxing gloves . . .)

FIGHTER
Hey . . . (arms brought forward, palms up) . . . Give me a hand.

(MAN stops assembling projection screen and

climbs into ring with water bucket. He checks
FIGHTER's face for bruises.)

You got a Fight Plan for me, Ol' Man?

MAN
Sure do.

(He takes boxing gloves off FIGHTER.)

FIGHTER
(impatiently)
Well? . . .

MAN
Well, what?

(MAN moves to FIGHTER's corner, places gloves
in bucket and sets bucket on floor.)

FIGHTER
(turns around exasperated)
The Fight Plan! . . . What's the Fight Plan?

(MAN takes sparring pads from bucket and moves
to center ring . . . FIGHTER, with hands still
taped, begins to bang the pads.)

MAN
Son, it's not exactly a Fight Plan.

FIGHTER
(stops sparring)
What do you mean, not exactly a Fight Plan?

MAN
(demands)
Keep working! Two jabs . . . a right . . . double
up on your left hook, then a right cross.

(FIGHTER resumes, follows instructions.)

It's more like a Life Plan.

FIGHTER
(still sparring)
What . . . ah . . . Life . . .

MAN
(interrupting)
Yes, a Life Plan . . . That'll do it.

FIGHTER
(sarcastically)
Do what? . . . (bangs with a hard left hook, then
stops)

MAN
(angered)
Don't stop working until I tell you! (FIGHTER
reluctantly resumes) . . . You want to whoop the
Beast . . . you got to have a Life Plan.

FIGHTER
(sparring)
A Life Plan.

MAN
Yep.

FIGHTER
(sparring)
Well, what the hell's a Life Plan?

MAN
It's the only way to kick Satan's a . . . Stand up to the Evil One.

FIGHTER
(sparring)
You mean the Beast.

MAN
No! I mean Satan. The Beast is a pimp . . . 'though he could mess you up a little.

FIGHTER
(stops sparring, backs off)
Mess me up a little?

MAN
Look . . . the one you got to get ready for is Satan. You get ready for him and you'll take the Beast . . . no problem.

FIGHTER
(disbelieving)
No problem . . .

MAN
(assuredly)
No problem . . . (holds pads up again for sparring) . . . Let's go!

FIGHTER
(sparring)
Well . . . ah . . . how . . . ah . . . how do I get this
Life Plan?

MAN
You work at it.

FIGHTER
(banging hard now)
When do I begin?

MAN
We're working at it right now . . . (drops his hands
and orders . . .) Do some sit-ups from the ring
apron. Keep moving.

(FIGHTER moves, bobbing/weaving. MAN
directs him over to ring corner, downstage right, as
MAN moves to opposite corner and places pads in
water bucket. MAN returns to FIGHTER.)

All right, let's do them.

(FIGHTER crawls under ring ropes and begins
doing sit-ups from the ring apron, arms crossed on
his chest as MAN holds his legs from inside the
ring . . . MAN counts. FIGHTER does 10–12 sit-
ups, then realizes he's outside the ring.)

FIGHTER
Hey . . . I'm out . . . I'm out . . . (stops doing sit-
ups)

MAN

Keep going, son.

FIGHTER

Don't you see, I'm out of the ring . . . I couldn't get out before, remember?

(FIGHTER tries to get up, but MAN holds hard to his legs.)

Let me go . . . The spell is off . . . I gotta get the hell outta here . . .

(MAN struggles with FIGHTER; kneels on his legs forcing him to remain.)

MAN

Don't you understand! . . . There's nowhere you can go . . .

FIGHTER
(not listening)

No . . . I'm out . . .

MAN

Listen to me . . . You can run but you can't hide.

FIGHTER
(disdainfully)

Who do you think you are . . . Ali!

MAN
(forcefully/slowly)

YOU CAN RUN . . . BUT YOU CAN'T

HIDE . . . (pause) . . . I'm going to let you go now . . . and you decide.

(MAN releases FIGHTER's legs, stands and backs off.)

Now, you decide!

(FIGHTER grabs ropes, ponders . . . slides under ropes out of ring.)

FIGHTER
What's there to decide.

(He moves further away from ring, stage left.)

I'm outta here!

MAN
And where you gonna go?

FIGHTER
Anywhere . . . just not here.

MAN
And what about the Fight?

FIGHTER
Screw the Fight . . . The deals off. This is too wild. I ain't gettin in that ring with the Beast anymore . . . and I don't want to see no Satan.

MAN

And what makes you think he don't want to see you.

FIGHTER

What do you mean?

MAN

I mean you called him out! . . . And you're going to have to deal with him one way or the other. You either sell your soul . . . or you fight him for your life. That's the D E A L! You just can't pull out from the Bout.

FIGHTER

(nervously)

Look . . . Look, MAN . . . I'm out, see . . . See . . . (walks around) The spells off . . . Deals off. That's it . . . See . . . that's it!

MAN

(disgusted)

I'm about done with you now, son. You're jiven yourself. The Evil One don't work that way. He don't play. You started it and he will finish it. Now you get yourself back here and train . . . or you can fight him without trainin . . . and without me.

FIGHTER

(confused, walks about . . . ponders)

This is crazy, Rocky. How on God's earth am I gonna fight such a power? It's not even human.

MAN

Trainin, son. We gotta build you up . . . Get you
a new attitude. Build your *mind* . . . your *body* . . .
and your *soouulll* . . . (pause) . . . and . . . we gotta
watch fight films.

FIGHTER
(surprised)

Fight films?

MAN

Sure . . . Now, if you'll get in here and do some
push-ups while I finish setting up, we can get on
with it.

(MAN exits ring and continues setting up projection screen as FIGHTER re-enters ring and does
push-ups.)

FIGHTER

How many do you want?

MAN

Keep going 'til I tell you to stop . . . (FIGHTER
looks disgruntled) . . . And face the projection
screen.

FIGHTER
(mumbles)

Projection screen . . . (as he positions himself toward the screen)

(MAN finishes setting up projection screen, enters
ring and takes out a clicker from the water bucket.

MAN walks to FIGHTER, who is still doing push-ups, and squats down next to him, but places one knee on top of FIGHTER's back . . . hard.)

MAN

Stop . . . (as FIGHTER is flattened to the ring floor)

FIGHTER

Ugh! . . . What the hell you doin?

MAN
(orders . . .)
Look at the screen!

(Stage lights go off; ring lights still dim as soft blue projection screen light is beamed onto projection screen.)

What do you see?

FIGHTER

I don't see nothin.

MAN

Look! . . .

FIGHTER

I'm lookin. I don't see nothin . . . just an empty screen.

MAN

You don't, huh . . .

FIGHTER

That's right . . . zero . . . nothin.

MAN

Well that's your life . . . Zero. You're a nothing!

(FIGHTER angered, tries to get up . . . MAN
pushes him down.)

You just keep lookin . . . (pause) . . . Yes, that's
your life . . . so far. Now, we've got to fill that life
in. Make it somethin to behold . . . Somethin
worth lookin at.

FIGHTER
(ridicules)
And how weee . . . gonna do that?

MAN

We need some close-ups . . .

(MAN presses clicker, blue light goes off/on as if
slide projector.)

That's it . . . (pause) . . . In the beginning there
was the light.

FIGHTER

Oh, Jesus . . . this'll take a year.

MAN

Shut your mouth, son, and pay attention.

(MAN presses clicker and slide projector effect
again.)

And in the end, there is the light.

FIGHTER

Is it over?

(MAN still squatting/kneeling on FIGHTER . . .
raises his arms to the heavens.)

MAN

God's light is never over.

FIGHTER

Right . . . Right . . . But is the screen light bullshit
over.

MAN

I know what you mean, son . . . And I'll say it
again . . . His light is never over.

FIGHTER
(exasperated, mumbles)

Geez . . .

MAN
(insistent)

Do you see the light?

FIGHTER

Of course I see the light . . . I'm looking right at
it.

MAN
And what do you see?

FIGHTER
(angrily)
Damn you, Ol' Man . . . I see the li . . .
(pauses) . . . Wait a minute . . .

(MAN moves off FIGHTER and kneels on ring
floor.)

I . . . I . . . feel that light. It's . . . it's beautiful . . .

(FIGHTER rises to his knees, looks toward his
stomach; perhaps a blue light now goes up on
him.)

It's in me!

(He turns to MAN and grabs him [pauses] then
says . . .)

It's coming from in me!

(lets go of MAN and looks at himself)

From inside me?

(searches for an answer, scared . . . grabs MAN
again)

What is this? . . . (demanding) . . . What is this
Light!

MAN

It is God . . . It is God within you.

FIGHTER
(yells)

I ain't no God!

MAN
(struggling)

Every creature has the touch of God within him.

FIGHTER
(lets go of MAN)

No! . . . No! . . .

MAN
(insisting)

Yes . . . It's true!

FIGHTER

For what?

MAN

To USE . . . To use for the benefit of others.

FIGHTER

But, I'm just a FIGHTER.

MAN
(infuriated)

No . . . You are more!

FIGHTER
I'm a PRIZE FIGHTER!

MAN
And you want the title more than anything else . . .

FIGHTER
Yes.

MAN
More than your life . . .

FIGHTER
Yes . . . Yes . . .

MAN
And you'd die for it . . . and you'd kill for it . . .

(FIGHTER begins to agonize/moan, holding his fists to his temples.)

You'd kill anyone and destroy anything for it . . . you'd stop at nothing, would you . . . even deal with the scum of the universe!

FIGHTER
Yes! . . . Damn you! . . . Yes!

MAN
Then look . . . Look at your soul . . .

(MAN hits clicker; red light hits projection screen, second red light on FIGHTER.)

FIGHTER
Aaaahhhhh . . . (as he grabs his stomach) . . . It's the Beast.

MAN
It is you . . .

FIGHTER
(in pain)
Noooooo . . .

MAN
You feel it within you.

FIGHTER
(holds his stomach and pleads . . .)
Oh! . . . God!

MAN
You are consumed with yourself . . . You want titles . . . You shut people out . . . You lock doors . . . So the Beast grows within you!

FIGHTER
I don't want it . . . Get it out of me . . . Shut that damn screen off!

MAN
It's yours with the title.

FIGHTER
(screams to the heavens)
I don't want the title. I AM NO BEAST!!!

MAN
Then what are you?

FIGHTER
(confused)
I . . . I don't know.

MAN
(insisting)
What are you! . . .

FIGHTER
(questioning)
I don't . . . (pauses) . . . Am . . . Am I mo . . . Am
I More?

(ring lights up full, red lights go off)

MAN
Say it . . . What are you!

FIGHTER
(confidently)
I am more!

MAN
Say it again . . . What are you!

FIGHTER
(raises his arms up and screams . . .)
I AM MOORREEE . . .

MAN
Believe it . . .

FIGHTER
(repeats)
I AM MOORREEE . . .

MAN
Make me believe it!

FIGHTER
I AM MOORREEE . . . MORE, ROCKY!

(MAN points FIGHTER toward projection
screen.)

MAN
Now look at that screen and tell me what you
see.

(blue projection screen light goes up)

FIGHTER
I see . . . (pauses) . . . I see me, Rock . . . But . . .
I'm old . . . real old . . . and I'm trainin young
fighters in the gym . . . *this gym!* . . . And they're
not very good. What does it mean, Rocky?

MAN

It means that's your life, son . . . (pauses) . . . But with NO Title . . . and NO Championship Belt . . .

FIGHTER

There'll be no press conferences . . . no TV coverage?

MAN

Not for you.

FIGHTER
(uncertain)

Hmmm . . .

MAN

You can still deal with Satan for the Title and become the Beast if you want.

FIGHTER

I ain't no Beast, Rock . . . (pause) . . . What about my fighters . . . will any of them be Champions?

MAN

You must make them all Champions . . . whether or not they win titles.

(FIGHTER stands, walks around ring contemplating.)

Do you understand?

FIGHTER
(long pause . . .)
Yes!

MAN
(firmly)
Do you want this?

FIGHTER
(at peace, smiles)
You bet I do!

MAN
Then you gotta fight to be more . . . to have what's on that screen.

FIGHTER
I'll fight, Rocky.

MAN
(stands and demands)
Will you fight for the Light!

FIGHTER
Yes . . .

MAN
Even if it means fighting to the end . . . with every once of life you have!

FIGHTER
Yes! . . . Yes! . . .

MAN
(joyously proclaims . . .)
NOW . . . you are worthy of looking at.

(MAN takes towel and moves quickly out of ring
through ropes, stage right.)

Come on . . . Come on now . . .

(MAN directs FIGHTER to the heavy bag on the
platform. FIGHTER is keyed up and moves
quickly out of ring to the heavy bag and begins to
bang it hard.)

Work it! . . . Work it hard! . . . Work it for your
life! . . .

(FIGHTER bangs bag with awesome hooks and
combinations.)

What are you?

FIGHTER

Light!

MAN
(repeats)
What are you?

FIGHTER
(still banging)
I am Light . . .

MAN

Who are you?

FIGHTER
(banging very hard)
I am more . . . I am more . . . More . . . More . . .
You bastard, Satan . . . More . . .

(FIGHTER repeats, each time he lands heavy
blows.)

MAN

That's enough . . . (FIGHTER keeps going) . . .
That's enough.

(MAN grabs FIGHTER from behind.)

You're ready . . . Take a shower.

(MAN throws towel on FIGHTER.)

Go on . . . Go on . . .

(FIGHTER, excited, runs the long way around
the ring from his position by the heavy bag to
downstage, across the stage in front of ring, then
exits upstage left. MAN moves into the ring to
pick up robe and water bucket, then exits ring.
When MAN reaches stage floor, loud sounds of
banging on the gym doors are heard. MAN looks
to one door and hollers . . .)

Stay out! . . .

(MAN turns/looks to another door, backs up to center stage in front of ring as loud, eerie, ferocious sounds are heard becoming progressively louder until MAN yells . . .)

Over my dead body! . . . You can't have him! . . . He will fight you!

(MAN turns about and about and yells . . .)

He will fight you, I say! He will fight you!

(Sounds are frightfully loud now, and MAN screams . . .)

HE WILL FIGHT YOOUUUU!!!

(MAN is sweating, shaking, pointing to one of the doors . . . After a few seconds, the sounds abruptly stop. Lights fade to dark.)

END ACT I

ACT II

SCENE IV

SETTING: No one is on stage. Stage lights are at ½. FIGHTER enters upstage left. He is dressed in pedestrian clothes . . . short leather jacket (collar up), pull-over shirt, dark pants, dark shoes . . . hands taped.

(FIGHTER walks near ring; soft music during monologue.)

FIGHTER

I never . . . ah . . . I never really talked to you before . . . (pause) . . . I'd like to try it now. See . . . I . . . I ah . . . got myself in . . . well . . . sort of a major jam and . . . I need your help . . . (quickly) . . . I know you've done a lot already . . . sending the Ol' Man here and all to train me and straighten me out. But . . . (digresses) . . . How do I call you anyway? . . . God? Jesus? . . . Hey, what color are you? I guess it doesn't really matter. What I'm trying to say is . . . ah . . . that I'm gonna get killed in that ring. That Beast . . .

he's so mean, and so damn big. The Ol' Man hasn't seen him . . . I have . . . and ah . . . I'm sure you have . . . No way in hell I'm gonna beat him. So . . . so I was wonderin if . . . well, now that I've seen the Light . . . if you could sort of change the odds a little bit . . . (quickly) . . . I'm not looking for you to fix the Fight . . . unless you want to.

(looks around, getting no response enters ring)

No . . . OK . . . no fix. But maybe if you can even it up a little . . . right now I gotta be a 100 to 1 underdog . . . Like I was sayin . . . he hits so hard . . . If you could . . . ah . . . just ah . . . soften him up for me . . . drug him up so he's wobbly . . . take some of his strength away . . . then maybe I'd have a shot at landing a few solid punches . . . (depressed) . . . before he kicks the livin hell outta me. (now more aggressive) . . . Look . . . Look . . . I know I don't deserve any specials favors . . . not believin in you and all . . . (angrily) . . . and making that stupid deal with the Devil. Ehhh. But . . . I renounce that. I'm through with him. I swear I am . . . and I'd like to get to know you. But, if I die . . . I won't get that chance . . . at least not here . . . and I don't know any place else . . . So . . . ah . . . whatda ya say . . . can pull some strings? . . . Can you do something for me?

(getting no response, sits on stool upstage left
corner, head down)

(After a time, FIGHTER hears a voice.)

Huh? . . . (looks up) . . . Huh? . . . You talkin to
me? (happily) . . . You're talkin to me! . . . (gets
off stool and moves forward) . . . How come I
made the deal in the first place? To get the
Title! . . . (apologetically) . . . Sorry . . . I know
you know that. What was the real reason? (ponders) . . . Weakness, I guess . . . wanted the easy
way out . . . the sure way . . . My FIX for life.
(agrees) . . . Yes, yes . . . you're right . . . he's a
dream killer . . . a hope killer . . . just wants my
soul . . . don't care nothin about me. (loudly) . . .
I realize that now . . . (corrects himself) . . . Oh,
I didn't mean to yell. (now whispers) . . . I just . . .
even up the odds a little . . . OK? . . . OK? . . .
(no response, he walks around the ring) . . . This
is hopeless . . . (leans on ropes and drops his head,
then . . .) What? . . . I've got a chance . . . What
chance?

(looks around and gets no answer)

Answer me, what chance? Hey . . . Don't leave
me . . .

END SCENE IV

SCENE V

(MAN enters stage left; moves to ring.)

MAN
Hey, son . . . what are you doing?

FIGHTER
(surprised)
Ah . . . nothin.

MAN
Well, come on . . . time to get dressed.

(FIGHTER exits ring and walks toward MAN. As
he gets close to MAN, another person, black,
enters stage left wearing a white tuxedo. He walks
between the FIGHTER and the MAN, and
says . . .)

PERSON
Excuse me . . .

FIGHTER

Who's that?

MAN

The Ring Announcer.

FIGHTER

There's gonna be a Ring Announcer?

MAN

Of course . . . Main Event, son. Come on, let's go.

(FIGHTER and MAN exit stage left. Ring Announcer enters ring; stage lights go down and ring lights go up full.)

(Ring Announcer is center ring with cordless hand microphone. All his dialogue will be very exaggerated as a Main Event Ring Announcer.)

RING ANNOUNCER

Ladies and Gentlemen . . . you are about to witness the *Ultimate Prize Fight* . . . a fight for *Mind, Body, and Soul!* The Marquis of Queensberry Rules have been dispensed with. This will be a *"fight to the finish."* There will be no 10 Count or saving by the bell. The combatants are in their dressing rooms in preparation and shall make their way to the ring momentarily. There will be no Tale of the Tape or introductions . . . because when these pugilists enter the ring . . . I ain't gonna be here.

(Ring Announcer sings the National Anthem . . .
"O say can you see," etc. After the National
Anthem, the Ring Announcer introduces the Fight
Announcer, white, who enters stage left wearing a
black tuxedo.)

RING ANNOUNCER (CONTINUED)
Ladies and Gentlemen, tonight's Main Event
Fight Announcer will be Mr. Don Durphey . . .
Ladies and Gentlemen, give him a hand . . .

(Fight Announcer moves into ring.)

RING ANNOUNCER (CONTINUED)
Mr. Don Durphey!

(Both announcers exit ring and move to upstage
ring apron area and sit before microphones to call
the Fight.)

FIGHT ANNOUNCER
Good evening, Ladies and Gentlemen . . . Welcome to this evening's Fight . . . And what a fight
we expect for you tonight. First of all, let's get a
little background information on our
FIGHTER from our color commentator, Mr.
Van Dale McClure . . .

RING ANNOUNCER
Ah . . . watch that . . . ah . . . colored stuff!

FIGHT ANNOUNCER
Sorry about that . . . no offense. But, seriously,

what can you tell us about the FIGHTER . . .
What do we know about him?

RING ANNOUNCER
The FIGHTER hails from West Virginia. He's
175 pounds with a 69 inch reach. He has a
record of 56 and 23 . . . that's not too good of a
record. Ah . . . his last bout was a title bout six
months ago and he got himself knocked out in
the second round . . .

FIGHT ANNOUNCER
And he got another title fight . . .

RING ANNOUNCER
Yeah . . . (laughing) . . . and he got another . . .
supposedly . . . another title fight . . .

FIGHT ANNOUNCER
I don't think he'll take it . . .

RING ANNOUNCER
Don't know, but . . . ah . . . he seems to be train-
ing real hard for this Fight . . . and here he comes
now.

(FIGHTER and MAN enter upstage left. The
FIGHTER, bobbing and weaving, is wearing a
purple robe with the inscription on back,
ROCKY'S FIGHTER. His boxing gloves, red, are
on and tied. He is wearing purple boxing trunks
with a white stripe. The MAN is wearing a purple
pull-over sweater which on the backside reads, in
white letters, *ROCKY.*)

FIGHT ANNOUNCER
Yes, Ladies and Gentlemen . . . the FIGHTER
has entered the arena . . .

RING ANNOUNCER
He looks in very good shape . . .

(FIGHTER quickly moves downstage in front of
the ring, then upstage right near ring bobbing/
weaving . . . shadow boxing.)

FIGHT ANNOUNCER
He's showing off his wind speed now . . .

(FIGHTER enters the ring at ropes stage right
near announcers. He continues shadow boxing
using the entire ring.)

The FIGHTER is entering the ring . . . Ladies
and Gentlemen, let's give him a big hand please.

(MAN is in the ring and stays near FIGHTER's
corner, upstage left, with towel, bucket under
stool; adjusts stool, etc.)

What do we know of the trainer . . . this Rocky?

RING ANNOUNCER
There isn't a whole lot . . .

FIGHT ANNOUNCER
Nothing we know of this Rocky.

(MAN gives pre-fight instructions to FIGHTER

who is still moving about ring. After a time, with
no sign of the Beast, the FIGHTER is befuddled
and turns to MAN and says . . .)

FIGHTER

Well . . . where the hell is he?

MAN

I don't know . . . maybe we scared it off.

(FIGHTER, center ring with back to opposite
corner, arrogantly acknowledges this possibility to
MAN . . .)

FIGHTER

Hey . . . he don't want me! He don't want me!

(However, the announcers are backing off in their
chairs, hands in front of their faces, terrified . . .
frightened because they see the Beast. The
FIGHTER notices the looks on the announcers'
faces. Still with his back to the Beast's corner, he
takes a step or two toward the announcers and
asks . . .)

What's wrong?

(All of a sudden, the FIGHTER is slammed to the
ring floor, face first, as a result of a heavy blow to
the back of his head by the Beast.)

FIGHT ANNOUNCER

Oh . . . Ladies and Gentlemen, did you see that
sucker punch. I've never seen anything like it.

(MAN rushes into ring and kneels over
FIGHTER. FIGHTER looks back across the ring
and, although frightened, nods his head acknowl-
edging that the Beast is here. The MAN under-
stands and quickly takes the robe off the
FIGHTER, who is still lying on the ring floor.
The MAN shoves the mouthpiece into the
FIGHTER's mouth and frantically yells to the
announcers . . .)

MAN

Ring the bell! Ring the bell!

BELL RINGS

(MAN quickly removes the stool and bucket from
the ring and stands outside the ring by
FIGHTER's corner.)

FIGHT ANNOUNCER

Well . . . welcome to the Fight, folks. Welcome
to Round 1.

(FIGHTER rises slowly, carefully watching the
Beast . . . He begins to circle counter-clockwise in
a stalking manner. Then, the FIGHTER taunts
the Beast . . .)

FIGHTER

Come on. Come on. (more loudly) . . . Come on,
damn you!

FIGHT ANNOUNCER

He's taunting him, Ladies and Gentlemen . . .

FIGHTER

You want me . . . (yells) . . . Here I am . . .

(FIGHTER throws a powerful right hand to the head of the Beast.)

FIGHT ANNOUNCER

Oh! . . . a wicked right hand to the head of the Beast . . .

(FIGHTER follows with a hard left hook to another head.)

What a start! . . . He follows with a left hook to another head . . .

(another left hook by the FIGHTER)

And, oh! . . . Another powerful left hook lands . . . Ladies and Gentlemen, I can't believe it but the FIGHTER has the Beast dazed . . . It looks stunned . . .

(MAN is yelling to FIGHTER.)

The FIGHTER's corner is yelling instructions . . . They want it over now!

MAN

Follow up! Finish it! Do it now! Do it now! Work the body . . . then move up . . .

(as FIGHTER throws a flurry of punches)

FIGHT ANNOUNCER

He's pounding the body heavy now . . . 20–30 unanswered blows . . . The Beast's mid-section is being pummeled. These are heavy blows, folks . . . The Beast is in serious trouble.

(FIGHTER works up to heads.)

. . . A left, a right, a left, left, another right . . . all flush in the faces . . .

(FIGHTER continues landing blows.)

And . . . this looks like an early knockout . . . an upset in the making . . . Perhaps the upset of the century. The Beast is just getting hammered. It hasn't landed a blow on the FIGHTER . . . (Beast swings) . . . Oh . . . there It goes . . . (FIGHTER ducks) . . . But It's just too slow . . . The FIGHTER ducks the punch; keeps banging away. Now the Beast moves away flailing windmill punches . . . but It misses. The FIGHTER's just too quick. Now the FIGHTER moves after It continuing his attack . . . and he catches It again with a jarring right hand . . . and his corner man is screaming . . .

MAN

Keep on 'im! Cluster punches . . . combinations . . . combinations . . .

(FIGHTER follows instructions, lands many blows.)

FIGHT ANNOUNCER
Oh! . . . again, a left, and a right, another right,
3–4–5 vicious hooks to the stomach . . . a hook
to the head . . . It looks like it will be over,
folks . . . only a matter of time . . .

(FIGHTER continues to beat on the Beast.)

The Beast looks beaten . . . legs are wobbly. It
should go down any second.

(Suddenly, FIGHTER backs off and looks over
the damage he's done.)

Wait . . . the FIGHTER's backing off . . . perhaps *he's* tired . . . so many punches. His corner
man is going crazy . . . imploring him on . . .

MAN
(screaming)
Don't let up! Finish it! . . . Go in for the kill! . . .
Don't stop!

(as FIGHTER moves in)

FIGHT ANNOUNCER
He's moving in now. The Beast looks helpless.
One more blow ought to do it, folks. It's only a
matter of time. FIGHTER stalks the Beast . . .
looking to unload the final blow. He moves in
with a left . . . Oh, my God . . . he gets nailed
with a vicious blow from the Beast . . . (sound
effects . . . roar/pow) that sends the FIGHTER

reeling across the ring. He bounces off the ropes
and he's down . . . Terrifying . . . a terrifying blow
caught the FIGHTER coming in square. Blood
is pouring out of his mouth . . . What a devastating punch. Caught him flush. The FIGHTER
is out of it . . . just out of it. He will never get up.
This fight is over, folks . . . What a reversal . . .

MAN
(yelling)
Get up! Get up! You can do it, son! Get up! You
can do it! You are More! The Light! Think of the
Light . . .

FIGHT ANNOUNCER
He won't get up . . . Ladies and Gentlemen, it's
just too much to ask. That should have killed him.
Look at him . . . he doesn't know where he is . . .

(FIGHTER slowly tries to get up.)

The Beast has remained in Its neutral corner
and . . . Oh, look at this . . . the FIGHTER is
trying to get up . . . I can't believe it . . . He's trying to shake off the cobwebs and . . . yes . . . he's
on one knee. Courage or stupidity, fans . . . I
don't know . . . but he's up on his feet . . .

(FIGHTER moves toward the Beast.)

And he's actually asking for more . . .

BELL RINGS

Well . . . there's the bell to end the first round, folks . . . and what a round it was . . .

(ad libs, volume down on Fight Announcer . . . MAN jumps in ring and brings FIGHTER to his corner.)

(FIGHTER sits on stool, semi-conscious.)

MAN

Keep away from It, son . . . keep your distance . . . make It move . . . It'll tire. You're smarter . . . faster . . . make It miss. You can't get hit square . . . work the jab . . . stick and move . . . stick and move. It's fat . . . out of shape . . . take the heart out of It, son . . . You can do it . . . with *this* . . . (points to FIGHTER's head).

And for God's sake . . . no peak-a-boo and no rope-a-dope.

(Bell rings for round 2 . . . FIGHTER gets up slowly; MAN moves out of ring.)

Stick and move! . . . Stick and move! . . . *Its got no heart* . . .

FIGHT ANNOUNCER

Well, fans . . . I don't know how he survived that blow . . . but here he is in Round 2. A game fighter he is. But more cautious now . . . much more . . . not quite as brazen . . . I don't hear any taunts from him. He's definitely not the aggressor. It seems like he's trying to keep his distance . . .

make the Beast come to him. Well . . . yes, that's the tactic . . . They're doing nothing at this point but circling the ring shadowing each other. Now, the Beast picks it up . . . It moves in and throws a telling left . . . then a right . . . The FIGHTER moves easily away . . . The Beast moves to cut off the ring . . . misses with a vicious right . . . FIGHTER moves to the side . . . gets caught with a glazing left hand to the ribs . . . hurts him . . . but dances away . . . The effects of even a glancing blow buckle the FIGHTER. The Beast is just too powerful. The Beast moves in again . . . misses with 2 lefts and a right . . . the FIGHTER is on his bicycle, folks . . . He's running. Well, who can blame him . . . Oh . . . the FIGHTER stops and delivers a jab then backs off . . . dances . . . now stops . . . 2 more jabs, now moves away . . . no effect on the Beast. It just keeps moving at the FIGHTER, quite clumsily I might add. But no question of Its superior power. And there's a jab by the FIGHTER . . . more dancing . . . nothing like Round 1, folks . . .

MAN
Keep your distance . . . Make It miss. Stick . . . stick and move. He'll tire . . .

FIGHT ANNOUNCER
Looks like the FIGHTER is just trying to survive . . . I guess he figured he gave it all he had in the first round and he couldn't put the Beast away. Again, the Beast moves in . . . a left misses badly . . . and, Oh! . . . a beautiful right hand

counter-punch caught the Beast . . . stops It in
Its tracks. Now the FIGHTER backs off and goes
back on his bicycle . . . The Beast appears out-
raged and lunges at the FIGHTER with a
right . . . misses . . . FIGHTER moves quickly
away . . . Beast follows . . . picks up the pace . . .
throws a left, and a right . . . left misses but the
right connects on the neck of the FIGHTER and
reels him into the corner . . . right above us . . .

MAN
Get out of the corner! Move out! Get away! . . .

FIGHT ANNOUNCER
The Beast moves in . . . the FIGHTER tries to
side-step but the Beast cuts him off . . . and another right hand by the Beast . . . connects . . .
and drops the FIGHTER in the corner like a
dead heap. Its punches are just too devastating.
The FIGHTER is hurt but conscious . . . he's just
sitting there . . . The Beast moves to the neutral
corner . . . The FIGHTER's corner man is shout-
ing instructions . . .

MAN
Get up! Come on! You can do it! Have to
move! . . . Stick and move!

FIGHT ANNOUNCER
I don't know what more he can tell him . . . this
is just a terrible mis-match, folks . . . Now the
FIGHTER gets up . . . apparently able to hear
his corner man's instructions 'cause he's back

dancing . . . WOW . . . 2 quick jabs connect . . .
slow up the Beast a little . . . FIGHTER circles
to his right and Oh! . . . a solid right hand to the
temple of one of the Beast's heads . . . and a
left . . . 2 lefts . . . 3 straight jabs . . . now combinations . . . The Beast counters with a left and a
right . . . missing . . . FIGHTER throws a left
hook to the body and moves away. The Beast follows . . . almost running after him. FIGHTER
moves away . . . dancing . . . He's running,
folks . . . They're both running. It looks like a
track meet in there . . . FIGHTER stops . . . un-
loads . . . 2 beautiful left hooks . . . a jab . . . another left hook . . . then he backs out, the Beast
in hot pursuit. Foam is coming out of the lion's
mouths. The Beast looks tired. The FIGHTER
is still moving/dancing . . . The Beast lunges . . .
and a right . . . misses badly . . . FIGHTER
counters . . . perfect left jabs . . . He's boxing
beautifully now. The Beast seems out of control . . . Its legs look heavy . . . guess not used to
all this moving around.

BELL RINGS

And that's the end of Round 2. A classic exhibi-
tion in boxing.

(ad libs, volume down on Fight Announcer . . .
FIGHTER returns to corner.)

MAN
See . . . you're out-smarting It. Stick and move . . .

jab . . . jab . . . counter with combinations. It can't keep the pace . . . How do you feel?

FIGHTER

I don't know.

MAN

All right, forget how you feel . . . Who are you?

FIGHTER

I don't know.

MAN

Yes, you do.

FIGHTER

Oh . . . Oh . . . I'm Light . . . More Light!

MAN

You're doing it, son . . . He won't last. I'm telling you . . . he won't last 8 rounds.

FIGHTER

Eight rounds? It hits me again, I won't last 8 seconds!

MAN

Don't get hit . . . stay away . . .

FIGHTER

Hey . . . I'm trying . . .

BELL RINGS

(FIGHTER gets off stool for Round 3.)

MAN

You're the Man . . . You're in *Control* . . . Remember that . . . You're in control!

(FIGHTER picks up chant as he circles the Beast.)

FIGHTER

I'm in control . . . I'm in control . . . I'm in control . . .

FIGHT ANNOUNCER

Here we are in Round 3 and the FIGHTER is picking up where he left off in the last round . . . dancing, moving counter-clockwise . . . But he seems to be mumbling something . . . Sounds like a chant . . . I can't quite make it out . . . Oh, he's saying he's in control. Well, we'll see. The Beast appears to be moving much slower at the start here . . . Oh . . . there it goes . . . moves in on the FIGHTER and connects with a left to the shoulder . . . The FIGHTER runs in pain. Now, the FIGHTER is yelling something to the Beast . . .

FIGHTER

You're a Pimp! . . . You hear me . . . a Pimp!

FIGHT ANNOUNCER

The Beast in furious . . . It charges the FIGHTER throwing lefts and rights . . . FIGHTER moves off the ropes . . . all missing . . . the Beast looks foolish. It goes after the FIGHTER again . . . FIGHTER stays center

ring and moves just out of the Beast's reach . . .
and Oh! . . . what a solid counter-punch, a left
stops the Beast . . . now a right, another right . . .
sharp combinations . . . The FIGHTER is just
unloading on the Beast . . . 15–20 solid lefts and
rights . . . all unanswered. The Beast is standing
there. I think it's out of gas. The FIGHTER backs
off and walks across the ring and lies on the
ropes . . . Yes, he's leaning on the ropes and appears to be saying something again to the Beast . . .
Can you make it out VAN?

RING ANNOUNCER
A cat or something . . .

FIGHTER
You're a pussycat . . .

FIGHT ANNOUNCER
What is it? Oh . . . he's calling it a pussycat . . .
(laughter by announcers) How do you like
that . . . a pussycat . . . Quite a pussycat. The
Beast is very angry, folks . . . and slowly moves in
towards the FIGHTER . . .

MAN
Get off the ropes!

FIGHT ANNOUNCER
The FIGHTER is still hanging on the ropes . . .
asking for it. The Beast lunges at the FIGHTER,
and Oh! . . . the FIGHTER moves inside the
Beast and lands a wicked right to Its head. He

spins the Beast around and shoves It against the ropes . . . Now the FIGHTER is flailing away . . . hard lefts, rights, lefts, rights . . . combinations . . . all connecting, folks . . .

MAN
Finish it! . . . Finish it! . . .

FIGHT ANNOUNCER
The Beast is helpless . . . It can't raise Its arms. It tries to get away but the FIGHTER shoves It back into the ropes . . . a right, a left, another left, a right . . . 3–4–5 solid punches . . . The Beast can't respond . . . and now the Beast trips towards the corner but the FIGHTER is all over It . . . hitting It on all heads. The Beast stumbles across the ring . . . The FIGHTER is just relentless . . . throwing combination after combination. He's got the Beast in his own corner and is hitting It with blow after blow . . . at will, folks. The Beast's hands . . . err . . . claws are down to Its side . . . The FIGHTER steps back . . .

FIGHTER
I'm in Control . . . Pimp! . . .

FIGHT ANNOUNCER
And now the FIGHTER is running up and kicks the Beast in his mid-section . . . Oh . . . again, and ah . . . twice . . . now again. Is this allowed, Van?

RING ANNOUNCER
I don't know . . .

FIGHT ANNOUNCER
The FIGHTER steps back and delivers an awesome right cross to the middle head of the Beast and . . .

(Silence . . . FIGHTER backs off. After a moment, the Beast falls to the canvas with a *thud* . . . sound effects.)

The Beast goes down! . . . Ladies and Gentlemen . . . the Beast is down! Flat on Its face—out cold! It's over folks! . . . It will not get up . . . What an upset! . . . An unbelievable upset! I can't believe it. What a fight . . . (ad libs, etc.)

(MAN jumps into ring; *victory* music.)

MAN
You did it! You did it! I knew you could . . .

FIGHTER
(hugging MAN)
I couldn't have done it without you, Rocky!

MAN
Yes . . . yes . . . we did it. It's over . . . It's over . . .

FIGHTER
Over . . . thank God, it's over. Yes . . .

(Just then, the most horrifying, frightening sound is bellowed out as the ring lights are bumped on/off.)

What is that?

(MAN is furious; speaks to someone.)

MAN
You can't come in here . . .

FIGHTER
(terrified)
Who . . . who can't come in here?

(rings lights still being bumped on/off)

MAN
(standing firm)
Get out of this ring . . . That's not the Deal!

FIGHTER
(backing up)
Who's in the ring?

MAN
Satan . . .

(Ring lights stay on; again horrifying, frightening
sound.)

FIGHTER
Satan? . . . I don't see no Satan!

MAN
He's for me to see . . . (to Satan) . . . Get out of
here! He defeated this trash heap . . .

(pointing to Beast on ring floor)

It's over . . . The FIGHTER is ours now. Yes, it's over . . . (yells) . . . GET OUT!!!

(Satan's horrifying sound is again bellowed out and MAN is instantaneously lifted off his feet and knocked backwards by a terrific force. He falls flat on his back on the ring floor, unconscious.)

(FIGHTER rushes to MAN, kneels over him.)

FIGHTER
Ol' Man . . . Ol' Man . . . say something. Come on . . . you're OK . . . You're not dead. Don't die. Come on . . . PLEASE . . .

(No response, FIGHTER pounds on MAN's chest to resuscitate.)

Don't die! . . . Don't die! . . . Don't die! . . . (pause) You can't die! . . . (cries out) . . . Nooooooo!!!

(MAN does not move . . . FIGHTER gently holds MAN's head then lays it down. In a rage, he gets up and screams at Satan, still unseen to him . . .)

I beat your Pimp! You can't do this!

(Another horrifying sound from Satan and, with a powerful force, the FIGHTER is knocked to the ring floor to his knees. The ring lights go dim and a strobe light goes up pulsating progressively faster and in sync with the action.)

I will not renounce GOD!

(FIGHTER takes a vicious blow to the face and
his head is flung to one side.)

Ahhhhh . . . (in pain) . . . I am Light . . .

(FIGHTER takes another blow to the other side
of his face and his head is flung the other way.)

I'm . . . Ahhhhhhh . . . Oh . . . geez . . .

(He takes more blows, now coming rapidly. In
severe pain, he cries out . . .)

I am MORE . . . Ahhhh . . . Help me, Jesus . . .
Ahhhh . . .

(Satan bellows out another horrifying sound,
which is now continuous. The FIGHTER, having
received so many blows is now on his hands and
knees. Then, he goes crashing to the ring floor . . .
face first.)

God . . . Help meeee! . . .

(Blackout)

(in great pain) . . . Help me . . . Help me, Jesus . . .

(After a few seconds, the horrifying sound stops
abruptly. The ring lights go up full . . . The MAN
and both announcers are gone . . . Only the

FIGHTER is in the middle of the ring. He
struggles to his knees and looks around.)

Ol' Man . . . Ol' Man . . .

(After a time, FIGHTER realizes his *VICTORY;*
appropriate Finale music here. Still on his knees,
he looks to the heavens . . . smiles, raises his arms
up in victory fashion and yells in celebration . . .)

yes, Lord!

(Blackout)

THE END

Script Notes

Script Notes

Script Notes

Script Notes

Script Notes

Script Notes

Script Notes

Script Notes

Script Notes

Script Notes

Script Notes

Script Notes

Script Notes

Script Notes

Script Notes

Script Notes

Script Notes

Script Notes

Script Notes

Script Notes